The A$$hole Manual

The Complete Guide to Understanding and Managing the A$$hole in Your Life.

Msss Jai

DEDICATION

For Mama. Thank you for all you have done. I need you so much. I am grateful for your being here.

For Daddy. If I could hug you just once more.

For Pooty. You'll always be my favorite. Go forth and be great!

Maxine Adams. Thank you for being there. Your wisdom is invaluable.

ACKNOWLEDGEMENTS

To my sisters out there, after reading this manual, if you find that the man in your life is not an A$$hole, congratulations! Please pass this information on to the countless numbers of women out there who must cope with an A$$hole every day.

To my brothers and friends, I pray you are healthy in your mind, body, and love relationships. If you recognize yourself in any of these pages, do your best to acknowledge it and seek help to correct your relationship etiquette. It all begins with your willingness to admit that you don't have all the answers. I'll be right here to assist you every step of the way.

Are you ready? Let's go!

TABLE OF CONTENTS

INTRODUCTION

WARNING:

This manual is not meant to male bash. It will give a glimpse into the mind of a man prone to selfish, disrespectful behaviors which would classify him as an A$$hole. You will see this word used frequently in this manual, so from this point on I will refer to the A$$hole as "AH", or "AHs", (apostrophe intentionally omitted).

My goal is to educate those attracted to this type of man about the damaging effects AH behavior has on their lives and how this negative behavior will sabotage any relationships they hope to build.

This manual is for you, whether you are currently dating an AH, getting over an AH, heading towards meeting an AH or avoiding a relationship with an AH altogether.

Use this book to help you to decode the AHs games, understand your role in the AHs life, and explain what your relationship with the AH will cost you.

Understanding AH behavior will help you confront your fears, and insecurities, make much needed changes to your thoughts, and feelings, and detoxify from the AH in every area of your life.

Please take your time when reading this manual. My suggestion is to read a few pages at a time. There is much information to digest, and you will want to ponder how your dating choices compare to those listed inside.

bad manners have been overlooked and gone without correction for many years. He typically has no idea of his wrongdoings. He cannot understand how or why his relationships continually crumble. Since he never learned the true value of a woman and how to respect her, he will flip in and out of mediocre situationships which gratify his lusts but have no real depth of intimacy.

In the beginning, the AHs love can be strong. He can make you feel like you have met the man of your dreams: deep conversation, passionate sex, exchange of common goals and interests. Much of this good behavior will come to a screeching halt as his inner beast begins to manifest. Over time, he will stop sharing his thoughts, and feelings. His goings-on will become increasingly secretive and shady. Honest, open communication will become null and void. He may begin to cancel plans at the last minute or without notice, make mean comments or put-downs, and find ways to convey his displeasure with the woman he claims to love. Yes, he may at some point say that he loves you, but don't hold your breath, he will only say these words when he is good-n-ready. Don't be fooled, confessing his love for you will only deepen your emotional bond with him. Proceed with caution.

Not Just the Money

Let's be clear, this manual is not just directed towards men with financial excess. The AH is not always a man with a great financial plan and significant resources. Finances can play a major role in why a man's ego becomes puffed up to the point of becoming an AH, but there are many AHs out there whose finances are excessively compromised (broke, busted, and disgusted). The AH type can come in all shapes, sizes, colors, and bank accounts.

The Purposeful Disconnection

The AH has made a conscious decision to please himself, and HIMSELF ONLY. His cleverly hidden, doggish mindsets stop him from connecting with his women EMOTIONALLY. An emotional connection will only make it difficult for him to leave when the time is right. He has mastered the art of disconnecting from the women he sees and will do so when he is bored and ready to play around. He will always keep his options open but will engage in a Purposeful Disconnection.

A Purposeful Disconnection is a hurtful technique the AH uses on a woman that will cause her to withdraw. His disrespectful behavior is designed to inflict mental and emotional pain on her. It is completely intentional and designed to trick her into submission. When she pulls away, he will run after her with a love-bombing strategy that no female can resist. She yields, returns and a cycle of abuse begins.

To solidify a Purposeful Disconnect, the AHs words and actions must become a source of continual pain. This will give him the distance and CONTROL he needs. This control will allow him to mold the relationship (and his woman) to give him maximum benefit and pleasure. His goal is to make her a "pleaser," fulfilling his desires whenever, and in whatever manner he wishes.

He has spent years perfecting this method of captivating women. They become accustomed to his zigzag style of love – hurt. Any lady who has passed his pain test (one who will stay with him no matter how badly he treats her), is an excellent candidate that he can fondle as he pleases.

Selfish

At his core, the AH is indifferent. Heartless. Cruel. These are strong words, but when his true character is revealed, you will find them to be accurate. He owes you nothing. You are lucky to spend time in his company. There are other women that he could grace with his presence. You are just a number. He has a No-Commitment Mentality which dictates that you pay HIM for his time and attention. He does not see value in women or relationships with women. Easy come, easy go. He sees nothing wrong with hopping from girl to girl and will do so without regard for your feelings, concerns, or well-being. Stop here and ponder your sexual health. If you have ever been sexually involved with an AH, get tested.

Unavailable

The AH truly enjoys your company, so don't expect him to completely cut you off when things get rocky. He won't. He could string you along for years, without a commitment.

He is emotionally unavailable by choice. He has already decided at present, that he will not love, commit, or marry. Even if he should find himself in either of these three relationship dynamics, he will half-heartedly put forth whatever effort is needed to keep you satisfied. He passes time by toying with females he won't devote to. He gets a strange satisfaction from dating and dumping even quality women. He believes another Bae is waiting for him, who is more worthy than you, of all he has to offer. He does not understand that good women are hard to find. He makes no distinction between quality women and rachet women. He treats them both the same. He is using them and all too often, the rachet ones are equally adept at using him for his money and whatever else they can get.

His Way or No Way

The AH is smart enough to know when to stop with his antics. Remember, he is an intelligent thinker and strategist. Do not be fooled; his schemes are designed to suck the life out of you with emotional ups and downs. He will do whatever it takes to maintain control. He wants to keep you in the realm of uncertainty, never knowing what you truly mean to him. You will ride the wave of his inability to commit and prioritize you in his life, and it will only make you crave him more. Your thirstiness makes him feel wanted and secure. His love bombing, love starving plan is training you to love him unconditionally – bullcrap and all. He has sized you up. He has figured you out. Groan and moan if you must. Ultimately, it won't do you any good.

He will willingly accept your confrontations. He will apologize for bad behavior because he knows it's what you NEED to hear. A true AH knows the art of a sincerely insincere apology. If your man exhibits AH behavior but cannot apologize, he probably falls more into the IDIOT category. We will talk about that in another book!

He will listen to your ranting and even change some of his ways to maintain the relationship. This does not mean he loves you or that he cares about a permanent relationship with you. He might refuse to let you break up with him because he knows his life is better off with you in it.

When he decides he is ready to cheat, he may (or may not) tell you up front, that he is seeing other women. Some AHs will continue to play with you until YOU give up hope that they will make you their number one and walk away. In this case, he checked out of the relationship long ago and was waiting for you to realize things were over.

Other AHs bore more quickly and are very impatient. After he has found a more exciting escapade to connect with, he will drop you like a hot rock to pursue his next victim - the one he had on standby while he was playing with you.

At the point where you prove that your health and peace are more valuable than your desire for his presence in your life, you deal him an ego blow that he will never forget.

Forget Your Heartache

The AH is counting on you to FORGET how broken-hearted you will be once you realize he has no plans to make you his one-and-only or future Mrs. Forgetting the pain he caused you is crucial to him continuing his bloodsucking tactics. He will want you to remain devoted and content in his web of confusion. When you forgive and forget, he will be able to carry on with the abuse and mistreatment. Holding a grudge will hinder his tentacles from lodging entirely into your heart and soul.

This is a great time to walk away from the relationship. It is here that you prove that your health and peace mean more than his presence in your life. Walking away will deal him an ego blow that he will never forget. AHs are always shocked when women finally wise up to their schemes and leave. Your departure is never anticipated, as he has invested much to be sure you leave only when HE is ready for you to go.

A true AH has a ruthless, prideful nature.
He is a hunter and a skilled warrior and cannot have
healthy relationships.

Alone and Lonely

Ironically, the AH would make a wonderful partner if he realized that time is short and opportunities for relationships can be wasted just like everything else. Countless women have walked away from him for his obnoxious behavior.

The older he gets the more the rejection will sting when it comes from a woman of value. Nothing is more sobering to the AH than being dropped by a woman that had her "ish" together.

A seasoned woman will walk away at the first hint of AH behavior. It will take much pain and effort for a rookie who has never fallen into the clutches of an AH to navigate through his drama.

As he ages, especially in his golden years, the AH will realize he missed out on women who truly cared for him. However, he may be so stuck in his ways that he will settle for whatever C or D-list woman that has fallen into his trap. At this point, he is either too old or too tired to continue the games. He might start to bend his ways as he comes to terms with the idea of spending the rest of his life alone, searching for authentic love. I have seen many men in their 60s and 70s finally figure out the changes they needed to make to move into healthy relationships. Better late than never!

If a man can repent, commit, and go on to be a great husband and wonderful father, he was never a true AH. A true AH has a ruthless, prideful nature. He is a predator and a skilled warrior. A true AH cannot have healthy relationships. His mentality and resistance to change hinder him from developing the intimacy and emotional unions he so desperately craves. Yes, he does crave true love, but his childish behavior and selfish habits will ultimately hinder him from building and maintaining quality relationships.

I hope that the AH will learn to lessen his harsh, narrow-minded ways and mellow out before it is too late. Perhaps after watching his children (if he has any) grow and experience the pain of failed relationships, he will realize that a selfish lifestyle can only push away the very people who were sent to love you.

The Single Life

The AH enjoys bachelorhood. When he gets lonely, he may ponder the idea of settling down, but as always, he will wreck any hopes of a healthy relationship with crude conduct.

He is not ready for marriage or any other serious form of commitment.

Being an AH is fun and exciting to him. He enjoys bragging to his boys about the many women he sleeps with. He and the bros can swap stories, tell lewd jokes, and pass around naked pictures and videos of their conquests. He loves boasting about his adventures.

Deep down, he longs for commitment, but his fear of missing out and his desire to play keep him chasing one petty relationship after another.

It would behoove any woman involved with him to pay careful attention to his actions and leave at first sight of any ill behavior.

A$$holes are not born.
They are made.
Through pain, privilege, and choices.

Chapter 2

THE PPC

The Pain

Past Pain.

Every AH has a past pain.

We can never be sure of what triggers a man's heart to turn towards AH behavior. A dysfunctional childhood? That girl who cheated on him and mistreated him? The way his daddy treated his mama?

It is difficult to speculate. The AH is not immune to pain. He was once the victim. What is familiar about this type of man is that he suffered a blow of rejection, ill-treatment, or a devastating love loss.

This man is ANGRY.

Every AH has a quiet-smoldering or deep-seated root of anger. He may be mildly mad, or mad, mad. He is angry with life, people, women, family, circumstances, or a combination of these.

Violations occurred where he felt taken advantage of. It rendered him helpless and catapulted him into an I-will-survive-I-will-get-you-back-you'll-see mental state.

His powerlessness in a season of hurt was a sordid recipe that created his perverted personality. He didn't get his way and in turn, he rejected the healing power of love that could have helped him to recover. He goes through life, dwarfed in his emotions, dragging his wounded soul with him.

His corrupt thinking and self-sabotaging habits allow him to behave without concern for how his actions make others feel.

He is an expert at camouflaging his hurt and resentment. This makes it barely detectable to those who are not diligently studying him. They lack the tools and insight to understand why he behaves like he does.

Whatever the cause of his love catastrophes, the AH has not recovered nor healed from abandonment. Perhaps it was an ex-wife or the girl of his dreams that he placed on a pedestal. He gave his heart and soul to her, and she used him, abused him, and then dumped him.

He compares this goddess to every woman he has encountered since she departed. In his mind, she was "perfect." You, my sister, will never measure up to this woman he desperately wanted but couldn't keep.

He trusted her and may never trust anyone as blindly. He carefully monitors even his sincerest lovers, with a sneaky level of hidden hurt and passive anger. His low-key lashing out is fueled by the bitter rejection from the princess of his past.

He may keep in touch with this woman, just to keep tabs on what is happening in her life. Perhaps he wishes they could reunite. My guess is he is still in love with her, but that is something the AH will never admit.

Tit for Tat

It has been said, "hurting people, hurt people."

The AH cannot help himself. His way of medicating his heartache is by inflicting hurt on others whether intentionally or not. He is hostage to his immaturity.

His response to conflict is tit for tat. If you wound him, rest assured, he will come back at you with vengeance. Beware any man who goes toe to toe with you when he feels violated in the simplest of situations. He is touchy and will find a way to get back at you, without you even realizing he was keeping score.

The Privilege

Financial surplus allows the AH to say and do with his women, whatever he is bold enough to get away with.

Who doesn't love a man with enough cash to whisk you away to weekend getaways and dinners out?

Be honest, how many ladies put up with an AH simply because of how much money he brings home each pay period or because of some good pickle? Add to this a nice body, and a handsome face and ladies turn into putty in his hands, ready for him to mold as he pleases. Our minds are busy daydreaming of red bottoms, designer bags, spa trips, stay-at-home wifey, or whatever lifestyle we can squeeze from his wallet.

The tradeoff? Living with his rude, obnoxious, and downright mean personality. Meanwhile, our self-esteem and self-worth erode bit by bit from the disrespect and the lack of love we experience while we wait for him to grow up. Many of us stay silent about this because this man meets our checklist, and we desire a relationship (even a poor one) more than we desire to be healthy. (Read that again.)

We spend months ignoring his disinterest, hoping things will somehow work out. Call his bad behavior what it is. Accept that this is what life will be like if you decide to stay in a relationship with him. If you put your foot down, and the AH cannot get away with stinky behavior with YOU - he will move on until he finds someone, he can have his way with. A closer look will reveal that he was never worth your time or attention. You were simply enamored by his social status, WEENIE, looks, or his ability to help you pay your bills.

The Choices

The AH will always make poor choices when it comes to the treatment of his female interests. He will choose AH behavior all the time and every time, even when circumstances dictate loving, affectionate responses.

He chooses disrespect.

He chooses to ignore your boundaries.

He chooses to coerce and bully you into following his directions.

He chooses to belittle your abilities.

He chooses to insult and demean you.

He chooses to insist that you meet his needs.

He chooses to ignore your feelings and how his treatment affects your well-being.

The list will go on and on. This man chooses to be an AH. This is what makes him the Kingpin of Dysfunctional Affairs.

He uses anger, pride, and ego as life compasses. His feelings and desires are always a priority, and mandate how he treats those around him.

It is always better to flee a man of this character at the first red flag you see. Ladies, your antenna should be on high alert for AH behavior. Do not ignore flags. It will save you time and tears.

How Does He Do It?

At some point in life, the AH discovers his knack for mesmerizing women.

Something about him is a valuable commodity within the female community and he uses it as leverage in the games he plays.

Whatever that element is, it affords him influence and control. Like kryptonite, this value weakens women, making it easy for him to get what he wants. He operates in a boldness which only an AH would display.

He developed his craft like a skilled musician. He is proud of his raw talent for manipulating and grooming those on his radar. He knows what his technique can do and how far it will take him. An expert player in the love game, he studies how to overtake his pawns with subtle precision to get them to fall for him quickly.

His resources enable him to easily invest in women without attaching his heart. CASH? Paying your rent? Cars and trips? Whatever his choice of payoff for you, it is designed to make you feel special, even though, in his mind, you are just the flavor of the month. It is only logical for you to think that he loves you since he spends his time and money to be with you. This is a façade.

JUST BECAUSE A MAN SPENDS HIS TIME AND MONEY DOES NOT MEAN THAT HIS HEART IS INVESTED IN THE RELATIONSHIP OR YOU.

He is unceasingly selfish, remember?

He knows that he must give to get.

He is used to "paying for the kitty", so he doesn't mind spending his coins to get what he wants.

He may treat you like his "LADY" one minute and the next cause silent tears that make your head spin.

He has an uncanny ability to envelope you in a fog of I want you – I don't want you, confusion. Add to this uncertainty the pain of no real commitment, and you are riding the AHs roller coaster of turmoil.

You are hoping for something permanent and healthy that will never manifest. Even if you win, you lose. His games are never worth playing.

Chapter 3

KINDS OF A$$holes

The Intellectual AH

This type of AH has a mixture of all the right attributes: articulate, resourceful, brilliant, grounded. Financially stable. Brains, beauty, body – or some other mesmerizing blend.

He is praised for his eloquent speaking and regarded as an expert for his shrewd ability to navigate complex situations - both in the office and in daily life. Others seek him out for advice and direction.

It is for this reason that this AH type worships his thoughts.

He believes he is more intelligent than the world around him.

He uses his intellect to control his environment and, of course, his women, and he gets away with it every time.

He's nice when he needs to be, but you'd better believe that he rules his kingdom with an iron fist and a do-what-I-say philosophy.

A woman who challenges his thinking and authority is rebellious and a problem starter. She must be TAMED and trained to yield to his thinking and manhood. He is, of course, more intelligent than she is. He is the "brain" and the "god" of the relationship.

On the flip side, this man is hypersensitive. He has deep wounds and is very insecure about his own identity. He is confused and depends on his intellect to uphold his self-esteem.

Life's daily ups and downs expose his tender confidence level. He will always be searching for a woman to follow his precise instructions. This boosts his fragile ego, alleviates his pain, and momentarily props up his shattered self-image.

The Broke AH

Let's be real; the broke AH does exist.

There is nothing wrong with a man saving his coins and finding creative ways to date that will save you both money.

Beware the man who will let you know up front that he is broke and that he just likes to relax on dates - at his place.

This man is not looking for love. He is looking for entertainment. Cheap entertainment that costs him nothing. What type of entertainment you say? Sex. All kinds and plenty of it.

Yes, you my dear, are his entertainment. Your body, specifically. Do not put yourself in the position to be used by this type of AH.

He expects sex. Period. He will tell you that sex is not important and that you can take your time to decide when you are ready, but sooner or later, he will want to get to the good part.

He expects you to offer your juicy free of charge and free of any strings, relationship expectations, or COMMITMENT. (Read that again.)

Don't expect dinner and a movie or a real date. In his eyes, him taking you out and spending his cash would mean that he would be paying for your spending time with him. Something a broke AH vows he will never do.

I'm not opposed to just chilling at home with my man, but this type of AH has NOTHING to offer except sex and is very shady and mysterious indeed. Dates with him are centered around his bedroom or TV areas.

The broke AH sees little value in women; but values significantly what her body can do for him and how it can make him feel. He steers his relationships with his peter and remote control - from his couch.

Mr. NETPHLIXX and chill. Sex is the date. The freakier, the better.

He may seem like a nice guy, but be warned, all it takes is a little time to discover that he exhibits classic arrogant AH personality traits. He thinks highly of himself and will expect you to cater to his every selfish whim.

When you fall in love with his soft side, you will discover (by accident) that his heart is under lock and key. He has no plans to really love you, or any other woman.

His focus (outside of sex) is on making it financially, and you can either help him or watch him as he scratches his way up. He has a plan for the females in his life and all it takes is one yes to help him make it. You are just the person for the job.

This man guards his heart with a steel cage. He will reward you for your time spent "chillin" with him with stellar sex. He has perfected his lovemaking skills so as not to disappoint.

THIS MAN IS A PLEASER. He will keep you on the sex wheel until your toes curl, your body shakes, and your brain implodes from his tricks.

Once he sees that you are okay with his "stay-at-home, sex-u-up financial plan", you will begin to loosen the grip on your juicy cookie. He will begin to push all sexual boundaries, exploring every aspect of pleasure. His goal is to blow your mind by exposing you to the super kinky and weird sex world, (and even better if you have already traveled there.)

His occasional flowers or trip to get your nails done will usually work to keep you believing that his heart is in the right place.

Would he ever ask you to borrow petty cash? Not likely. This type of AH is too proud even to consider begging you for a dime, but an occasional pizza or dinner and drinks on you is welcomed.

He will talk of marriage; to snare your heart, but his real interest is in how much credit he could get if you agree to co-sign for that new equipment or truck that he needs for his umpteenth get-rich business idea.

So, there you are, in a full-blown freaky situation, with a man who has nothing to offer you. Except. Good. Sex. And you are okay with that since he has shown you that he is working on a business plan to better himself and his finances. He only needs you to help him with your 700+ credit score and signature.

This AH has learned to market himself in a way that allows his chauvinistic behavior to be overshadowed by his talents. What talents are those, you say? His amazing oral sex and lovemaking skills, good looks, sexy body, false loving demeanor, charm, manliness, and calm listening ear. All of these become more important to you than his ability to take you out to dinner and to buy you trinkets.

He has become an expert at all those intangible things you crave from the men who have the cash - but are too selfish, too distracted, or too stupid to realize you need. Those missing elements can be mesmerizing to a woman who has been starved of them for any significant length of time. The broke AH is ready to take full advantage of your hunger.

Be careful when pursuing a romantic relationship with a man whose finances are sketchy. This AH won't attempt to court you and take you out on dates. There are plenty of events that are free of charge and, with just a bit of planning and creativity, can make for a fun evening. If he were truly interested, the broke AH would make the effort.

You must scrutinize this man's motives. Is he simply looking for a sex toy or on the come-up and looking for a sponsor? Ladies, our goal is not to use or abuse a man's finances, but we must avoid at all costs the broke AH and the traps he orchestrates.

Why would a woman pursue a relationship with an AH of this kind?

Her willingness to settle for whatever crumbs he audaciously feeds her, and her thirst to be held, validated, or sexed drives her to cling to momentary happiness in his arms.

Their chemistry and sexual connection feel good, but it is a trick and a coverup. He is offering something she desperately desires that feeds her mind, body, and soul. She will risk her health and peace of mind to stay connected to him.

Both parties are to blame, but she has not dealt with her brokenness and embraces what will silently destroy her. He is a user, a manipulator, and a liar, pretending to love and cherish her.

My sister, we must say NO to unhealthy relationships that only drag us down and hinder our growth. Even if you share amazing chemistry with this type of man, don't get it twisted. He is still an AH in every way. His selfish nature is in full throttle. Women are willing to forego what is most important - his desire and ability to PROVIDE, respect, COMMIT and love them because he is gifted in OTHER areas.

The broke AH is even more brazen and chauvinistic in his technique than any other AH type. He will stoop to the lowest levels of disrespect, out of his cesspool of experiences of sexual depravity, financial desperation, and misery. His mean, grinchy personality stems from a lifestyle of lack, a barely-getting-by mentality, and the failed relationships he has been subjected to again and again.

I have counseled this type of AH. Life has dealt him a very cruel hand. Perhaps if his responses were different, and his faith in God were in operation, he could overcome mentally and spiritually. Not only is his pocketbook bankrupt, but his soul is equally bankrupt.

Stay away from this type of AH. He will only take from you. Never open your financial resources to him. He is a user of the worst kind and will deplete you emotionally even if you don't offer your coin purse to him. He will spend very little of his resources to show you he cares but will overcompensate with thick love bombing and rope and chain sex strategies that are designed to trap you into never leaving him.

His goal: he will do whatever it takes (for how long it takes) to see you sexually strung out. His tricks are designed to feed your soulish realm with a pleasure you have only dreamt of.

After he has addicted you to his style of passion, he will enlist you to join his team of personal whores and threesome candidates. Don't believe for a minute that he will ever love you only. This man is so broken that he will boldly sell you his desire for love triangles and sister-wife relationships.

With him, anything goes - but only after he has reprogrammed your mind to accept his twisted group sex-love doctrine. Do not fall into his trap. It is a level of mind and soul control orchestrated by the devil himself.

Run my sister. Do not walk. RUN away from this AH type as fast as you can.

The Winning AH

This AH has a proven track record of success in his personal life and the workplace. He enjoys being able to maneuver amongst circles of champions.

He is witty, talented, and polished. He makes quality decisions (except in his love life) which work favorably for him. He walks in the upper echelon of the "bruhs," and they look up to him as the ultimate modern-day pimp.

He is known for his smooth demeanor and his game with the ladies. He is perfectly comfortable with being a boss and does a great job of it. He does what he wants, when he wants to, with no excuses, apologies, or explanations. Money and accomplishments make him feel valuable and accepted. His conquests with women make him feel like the winner he thinks every man should be.

On the flip side, his many insecurities make him desperate for acknowledgment and attention - even more reason for him to excel in his conquests with the ladies.

Every win with females feeds his ego. The more he wins, the more manly he feels. The more manly he feels, the more ladies he adds to his roster, and the greedier his itch for more games, power, and control.

He is trapped in a vicious, self-destructive cycle.

The Combination AH

There are many men out there who possess a sliver of AH characteristics, that are not full-fledged AHs. These men have varying amounts of AH traits, 10%, 20%, or more. It can be extremely frustrating to the woman in his life to decipher if this man is worth maintaining a relationship with.

AH behavior of this type is difficult to predict and not always displayed. This is the kind of man you fall in love with who gives few if any warning signs. You will discover, later in your relationship, that he is broken as trouble begins to manifest. This type is the perfect gentleman, until he feels disrespected, taken for granted, or let down in some way. His temperament can change from sugary sweet to ugly in a flash, making you wonder if he has an undiagnosed Bi-Polar condition, or if he is mentally ill.

Of all the AH types, this is the most common and by far the easiest to maintain relationship with. Many women press onward for years in relationships with a Combo AH. Sometimes he behaves like a nut, sometimes he doesn't. His good may outweigh his bad, and in that case, my advice to you dear sister, is to hang on in there. However, if his bad outweighs his good, then you know what to do! Run!!

Chapter 4

THE GAMES THEY PLAY

If he feels he can't control you,
he will walk away from you.
AH pride will mandate that he always comes out on top.

The Games They Play

Men play games. The AH is full of them. He is a master game player.

You must understand this crucial fact regarding his personality. He has a calm, wicked demeanor carefully hidden behind a tantalizing smile that is highly deceptive. Don't be fooled by his good looks or charm.

He derives pleasure from seducing women, but his seduction ploy does not always end in sex. It ends with him getting what he wants: CONTROL. For him to lose control is an insult to his manhood.

No man wants to feel like a loser, particularly an AH, and especially to a woman.

His MO (modus operandi) is to WIN - at all costs. His pride will mandate that he comes out on top. He will walk away from you early in the relationship, if he feels he can't win and control you.

For a woman to exist in his world, she must have a certain level of surrender in her soul. She must give up her power and yield to his manliness and authority. She must let him lead, even though he is misguided and terrible at it. He will have it no other way.

The AH will not stick around with a woman that he feels he cannot dominate and be "in charge of." This is especially true of issues that are important to him - whatever those may be, such as money, intellect, or athletic ability.

AHs purposely choose women they can feel more powerful, smarter, and wealthier than. He is a CONTROLLER. Naturally, he wants to be the authority and the greatest influence in your life.

No man wants to feel like a loser,
particularly an AH,
and especially to a woman.

Ownership and Dominion

The AH wants to feel a level of ownership over his woman, as many men do. He wants to feel as if your honeypot belongs to him and him only.

I have heard that a woman's heart resides in her honeypot (vagina). Once the AH feels he has control over your honeypot, (that he has total access to it whenever he desires), then he has dominion over you.

His goal is to dominate. When he feels that he "owns" your honeypot; and that you won't withhold it or deny him, his goal to dominate you has been achieved.

The AH wants to put you in a position of total submission, not just sexually. Once he has achieved total submission from you, he will say and do whatever it takes to maintain this power. He desires to control the deepest part of who you are - emotionally, mentally, and physically.

He may verbalize ownership of your privates, but it is only a mind game and means nothing to him. He can simultaneously spew these words out to you, Chante, Cathy, and Jodi.

Your honeypot is a gateway to your heart and soul. The AH knows this and will strive to possess you in these areas first.

His sex with you is sacred. He will use it against you to bind your soul to his. He will find some way to manipulate you, to keep you coming back to him for more. Some women he will sexually starve. Others he will sleep with frequently. His tricks are limitless. Beware!

An old man's advice to a young
man on dating and being a playa.
Get her mind first... her body will follow.

Unfaithful

The AH will always expect you to be cool with him tramping around and sexing you too.

Some AHs will confess their infidelity outright; others, may never be honest and swear they are loyal to you – even when blatantly exposed.

The AH feels that he has a right to cheat. He feels entitled. If he never agreed that he would have sex ONLY with you, and you are okay with this, then you have given him permission to play the field.

If he never committed to you, then the two of you are merely "spending time together," or "just hanging out". He has a legal right to date and have sex with other women. He never said he would be loyal to you in the first place. His lack of commitment conversation is intentional. It will allow him to steer the direction of your relationship, so that he can sleep around with whomever he pleases.

The pain of being number 2 or 3 is never worth your time. The AH will continue playing around with other women knowing he is your first choice. His refusal to reciprocate by putting YOU first is a heartbreaking stab of rejection. My advice to you is to move on. Do not allow yourself to become the tag-a-long girl, waiting for the AH to pick you, from the many women he runs through.

Some ladies avoid the "what are we" conversation because they do not want to seem pushy, desperate, or like they are trying to pin a highly sought-after man down. Please do not avoid this conversation. Tackle it head-on. You deserve to know the direction your situation is headed in.

Remember, a girl like you has OPTIONS.

Together, but Not Committed

The no-commitment issue is a huge red flag and should never be tolerated. Do not stay in a relationship with a man who refuses to define his role and status in your life, cheats on you, or plays foolish games.

You are committed to him, but in his eyes, you are simply his bae, girl, or boo. What you have, my friend, is a committed relationship with no real commitment.

Never permit this treatment to exist. Call it the abuse it is. A little abuse is still abuse. Do not waste your time with a man like this.

If your relationship lasts three months, you will have a glimpse of this man's character. Long before month three, you and he know if the other person is someone worth pursuing a relationship with. Some people think they need more time to figure out what they want to do. Three months is plenty of time, and any longer than that is a waste of energy for both people when red flags are glaring.

If a man cannot commit to a relationship within three months - you have your answer. The three-month cut-off rule is a safety net to prevent prolonging a dead-end relationship. The AH will never be honest about his lack of interest in you. If he cannot commit at the three-month cut-off, DUMP him.

Remember, a girl like you has OPTIONS.

Healthy Power

There is a fine line between healthy power and abuse that a man can have in your life.

A healthy alpha male will want to be in charge. There is nothing wrong with that. Women want to submit to a man in power who knows how to lead, nurture, and support them. The tricky part is his balancing authority, respect, and power without using any of the three to dominate you.

Healthy power and control in love relationships have boundaries that end when pain or discomfort begins to manifest. Fear, guilt, shame, pain, embarrassment, and humiliation are signs that your healthy power and control have been violated.

The AH is a power whore and has no regard for healthy boundaries in his love relationships.

*Many women do not understand
how they became trapped in the AHs snare.
Let me explain it to you.*

Playing the Role

You played the role he assigned to you. You stayed in your place. He set boundaries for you in his life, and you happily agreed to his terms.

For good reason. This is not a man you want to lose. This man is a good catch, and you don't want anyone else to have him. He is the total package. Prosperous, hardworking, intelligent, affectionate, and funny. He is everything you want in a man. Minus the issues that you are sure can be worked out over time. The smell of his cologne and thoughts of him still make you dizzy. Don't even mention the size of his woohoo or his sexual expertise. The "connection" between you and how he makes you feel when he puts it down seems worth the sting of rejection when he ignores you or keeps you waiting – alone.

Do you see the trap? You gave too much too soon. Available. Helpful. Doing. Being. Submitting. Meeting his needs, sacrificing your own.

You perceived him to be a quality man, so you gave him your best self. This is a mistake that many women make. Never give your best self away freely. Your best self must be earned! Your time, beauty, BODY, kindness, attention, SECRETS… your ish!

For all his positive qualities and the cash in his bank account, you decided you would put up with his relationship wackness.

Never mind the nasty, rude things he says or does that hurt and offend you. They seem trivial compared to all his positive qualities. Don't forget the SUBTLE yet OBVIOUS red flags you chose to ignore. The ones you overlooked because you felt this man was WORTH IT. There is, after all, something wrong with every one of us, right?

Okay, maybe you did none of these things. But you still put up with his disrespect. Nice, easy-going, non-demanding, sometimes a lil petty, (but that's okay, nobody's perfect), you.

There are good times, the sex is fire. You can't get enough of him. You allow yourself to fall in love. And fall hard, you do. But there are those moments when he just does @#%!. He acts-a-fool, and you must be honest and admit, that this man is an undeniable AHoleeeeee, no ifs and's or buts about it.

And.
Yet.
You.
Stay.

Chapter 5

WHY DO WE STAY?

Many ladies stay with the AH because they believe he will eventually commit to them and behave as he should. What they fail to understand is that the AH is only maintaining the relationship for selfish reasons.

He is USING you.

He will be your friend, lover, and whatever else for as long as he gains from you and for as long as you can keep his attention.

The two of you have a great "connection"? The closeness you feel is not authentic. It is a lie, a fantasy, a dream. It is your fierce loyalty to him, tolerance of his low-key disrespect, and your willingness to stick around to endure all the dung he dumps on you. The undeserved freedom of your juicy that you grant to him whenever and however (and whenever) he pleases. Simply put, darling, YOU are connected, he is NOT.

He loves the access he has to you - your body, time, and energy.

He knows he has a special place in your heart. You are EASY to talk to and to be around. He can always come to you for soul nourishment and some good lovin'. He can easily coerce you into doing the sex tricks he loves. You rarely, if ever, deny him. You have a tough time saying NO, but when you do, he can quickly change your mind by seducing you, as only he knows how.

Of course, you decided to stay. Not only do you stay, but there you are. Dreaming of the wedding, on the beach. The dress, the ringgggg, the bridesmaids. THE HONEYMOON! And you think, it's about time!" You breathe a sigh of relief and smile to yourself at how happy and lucky you feel at this very moment. God is good!

And then it happens. He does his usual AH routine interrupting your blissful fantasy of what could be. What the $#@% is wrong with him? Why can't he just act right?

The Answer is Simple

He cannot just "act right" because he is an A$$HOLE. An A$$SHOLE will do what an A$$HOLE will do.

He must stick to his script. He will not deviate. He will not change.

The sooner you understand and believe this, the more quickly you will be able to protect yourself from his whirlwind of dysfunction and his never-ending cycle of abuse.

Even when you put your foot down, stop spending time with him, and refuse his phone calls, he will continue to hit you up on social media; or show up on your doorstep or job, looking for an opening to continue this "thang" that you and he share.

Ladies, please do not be fooled into staying with a man who does not celebrate your value.

How Did I Get Here?

You dove in, full speed ahead.

You knew in your heart, that a relationship with this man was RISKY from the beginning. From those early first signs of disrespect - the ones you ignored.

Defying all reasoning, logic, and common sense, you gave him time to straighten out his issues and work on his behavior. You hoped for the best and stayed positive.

You weren't trying to change him. You were working to establish healthy relationship boundaries. You confronted him and told him about his errors. He seemed apologetic, and you grew closer and made real progress.

He was receptive, and you could see he was trying, and so you continued, thinking things would turn out okay. You became a regular fixture in each other's lives. Days, weeks, or months have gone by. Now, you are nervous and wondering, when will this whatdowecallthis turn into something? Why hasn't he said anything about us? WHERE IS THS HEADED?

You don't want to press him to discuss your future just yet. You are hoping he will bring up the topic on his own soon. You play the waiting game and pep-talk yourself into a state of complacency.

Meanwhile, the AH; has his own plans.

Plans to see just how far he can string you along.

Plans to see how much he can get away with - with as little effort as possiblc.

Plans to see how deeply he can get you to love him no matter how badly he treats you.

Plans to see how much control he can exert over you, your thoughts, your emotions, and your life.

The big question is how long will it take for the AH to end his AH ways? When will he truly share his heart with you (or any other woman)?

Here is Your Answer

Understand that the AH may never come around. He is a man-child, and his life revolves around the ridiculous behavior he loves to engage in. Please realize that even if the AH has committed to you, his crooked values of women will always be a stumbling block to the healthy respect you long for.

A title or ring will never change his mental capacity to love, honor, and care for you as he should.

I don't know which is worse.
an AH who will never clarify your status in his life,
or
an AH who will call you his gf,
little lady or significant other
and still act a plumb fool.

Chapter 6

WHOSE FAULT IS IT?

Are we ladies to blame?

Are we enablers, prompting the AH to take our kindness and love for granted?

Let's be fair. We give too much, ask for too little (or nothing), ignore warning signs, and consent to vague, halfhearted situationships without any formal promise or commitment.

Even if we are given a commitment, we consent, often silently, to pathetic relationship standards. Usually, we know deep down in our hearts when we need to walk away, but we think with our emotional honeypot instead of our logical left brain.

Wisdom tells us that the AH is arrogant and abusive. That he treats us like an accessory he can pick up and put down whenever he pleases. That he won't engage in a real relationship with us no matter how much we love him, how nice we behave, or how good our sex is. If only we would listen to the voice of wisdom. We would save ourselves much heartache and sorrow.

Ladies, be honest. If the AH treats you in a way that is painful and displeasing, why do you stay?

Is it because of your brokenness and fear of finding a quality man? Is it because you finally met someone with something going for himself instead of the usual clown who wants you to "mommy" him?

You must pinpoint why you are attracted to this man and what inside you desires to CONTINUE to be with him – even when he is a source of pain for you. You must recognize the AH for what he is. An A$$HOLE! He may be the catch of a lifetime, but the misery that will come with him will be more costly than your soul can afford.

Why? Why? Why?

Perhaps your version of AH has none of the previously mentioned traits. His behavior is perfect, but he refuses for whatever reason to commit, and days turn into months, and years of waiting. Why?

He is not ready.

He is not mature. He is emotionally damaged, selfish, and unwilling to change.

The AH will require that you wait for him to get ready for a commitment. He feels like something better than you is coming, and he doesn't want to miss out on it by tying himself down. This works for you; since you have eagerly agreed to stay and submit to his relationship tomfoolery.

This man will continue to waste your time, energy, love, and life. He will string you along, break your heart for sport, and refuse to let you go.

You have not had the epiphany, but he is not confused about his strategy to use you. Your best option is to remove yourself from his venomous fangs and pursue the healing that you deserve.

Help! I'm Stuck!

If you are stuck with, married to, or share children with an AH, there is help for you.

You likely surrendered your power to his demanding temperament long ago. He is used to the foundation of control he has established in your relationship. What you must do now is reclaim your personal power and begin setting new boundaries that will minister life to your injured spirit.

Keep reading. We have included an action plan that will help you.

The Wakeup Call

The AH showed you who he was from the very beginning. He lacks the self-discipline to honor women as the beautiful creatures God formed them to be.

He is used to getting his way.

A dishonest predator, he knows that a quality woman like you, requires something from him. He will willingly comply. But only for a little while.

He's an AH, not a nitwit. You are, after all, special. He is aware of your value as a woman, but he does not respect your value as a woman. He knows just how much to give you, to stop you from finding another man. He will work overtime and double time to keep you trapped. He will hide his character deficit and poor relational skills with trinkets, gifts, or spicy sex. He will make up for his poor treatment of you with tainted displays of affection.

He knows that he is an AH. Many women have called him by this name.

You cannot leave him. He is a winner. Winners stay on top. You cannot leave until HE says you can. He will want to leave you first. From the beginning, he aims to win you over before you discover what a rotten snake he really is.

Chapter 7

THE 13 BIGGEST MISTAKES WOMEN MAKE WITH A$$holes

Mistake #1
Wanting or Expecting More.

Let's face it, women want unconditional love. Women want honesty, intimacy, and sex. Women want commitment, but what makes a woman want more from an AH, knowing that doom may be lurking in her future?

A woman wants more from an AH because she loves him. She believes that the lifestyle she will lead once he is committed to her will be worth all the pain she has endured on the journey to get there. Ladies, wanting or expecting more from an AH is a waste of your time.

The AH has predetermined what he will give you, and it will never be what you are longing for. The desire to be with an AH is not always about money. Status may also be a key ingredient. Whatever the reason, expecting love in return is a big, fat lie. Many have blindly followed their hearts and given their love without measure to this type of man. We must stop hoping for what could be and take our relationships at face value.

Some of us are in Love with Love. We dream constantly about being someone's significant other or Mrs. We cannot wait for that chapter of our lives to begin, but is it worth sacrificing our self-respect and emotional health for? Never. Even if you have been married before and are over the thrill of running down the aisle, you may still crave intimacy, companionship, and want more. Prayerfully, you will find it with someone who will partner with you in life and love you unconditionally.

Meet Kelsie, 31, from Knoxville, TN.

"We've all been there. I am guilty of wanting and expecting more from a man that I knew was an AH. I knew he wasn't treating me the way I deserved to be treated. Yet I still wanted all of him.

Perhaps my brokenness and not wanting to be alone drove me to cling to a man who only gave me a piece of his heart. Or maybe it was the life I dreamt that we could build together. Maybe it was the fact that all I ever dated before him were bums with no drive, no discipline, nothing to offer me. No money, no vision, and an astute desire to take, take, take from me. This man had money, charm, and good PICKLE. I was willing to take my chances, and I paid a huge price. Learn the lesson, ladies. It's never worth it."

Mistake #2
Expecting the AH to commit.

A commitment was never in his plan. The AH enjoys managing multiple women. Why would he commit to one woman and limit his sexual and emotional freedom?

He will always put his feelings and desires above yours, causing you great distress. He will always engage in juvenile behavior that makes you question his love for you. All the good that he does will never outweigh the continual disappointment that he will bring into your life. He will consistently hold back and be distant because it is his nature to do so. When you are tired of guessing where you stand with him, he will find a way to continually avoid exclusivity and intimacy. This man has no desire to discuss relationship details. He knows that he has no intention of making you anything but a side piece in his life.

If we are honest, a relationship is good or bad for us. We are either committed, working towards a commitment, or wasting our time waiting for a commitment from a man who does not realize our worth. The AH will do what he wants. You can either wait and suffer or walk away and find the love you deserve.

Mistake #3
Expecting the AH to be Loyal

The AH cannot be loyal. He plays the field for jollification. He is a modern-day panderer. He is on the continual hunt for a slave that will give him whatever he desires. The only thing he is loyal to is his own agenda. He will never stop his wangling ways. His heightened boredom disorder drags him like a ragdoll to whoreish habits and behaviors. I have counseled many women who dated and married an AH they felt they couldn't live without. He repeatedly took them for granted, cheated, and caused them much grief. Relationships of this kind typically end in divorce, or worse, the couples are still married and miserable.

This man will never be loyal.

Mistake #4
Expecting the AH to treat you with the respect and dignity you deserve.

The AH does not respect women.

Why?

Fear, hurt, pride, rejection, chauvinistic traits passed down from male family members, and sexist societal norms are just a few reasons. For the AH to respect women would mean that he would have to change his wicked ways. He may need to forgive the women in his past and his mother may be on the list. Changing his ego-driven, self-seeking habits is not something he feels he needs to do. He deserves to treat women the way he does, and to be treated like the king he is.

Consider the men you know who treat women as they are supposed to be treated. They have a healthy respect for themselves that allows them to see women as valuable creatures with opinions and feelings that matter. The AH feels there is nothing wrong with his behavior and there is no need to consider changing.

Mistake #5
Expecting the AH to recognize what a great catch you are.

He knew from day one that you were a great catch. This means nothing to him. He will play with trifling women, but he is genuinely attracted to quality women.

The AH is not looking for a girlfriend. He is not looking for a wife. He is not looking for a commitment. He is looking for a toy, a playmate, and a good time. An experience. A tramp. Someone whose self-esteem is low enough to let him have his way.

Acknowledging and confirming your worth and treating you accordingly was never part of his agenda.

Mistake #6
Ignoring flags that prove he would make a terrible husband or life partner.

Come on, my sisters. You saw the flags. You kept going. You wanted that man. The little impulses you get tell you what is to come. God has a way of showing you what you need to see to help you stay safe.

No. It won't be okay, no matter how badly you want it to be. This man is a snake and will not morph into Mr. Wonderful. Don't dismiss the flags meant to save you from pain and torment. Put yourself first. Work harder to SAY NO and walk away. The longer you stay in an abusive relationship, the more normal the abuse becomes and the weaker you become to resisting it.

This is why it will be harder for you to leave, even when you are beyond ready to get out.

Mistake #7
Dismissing the pain, you feel when you are being neglected, ignored, and taken for granted.

Abusive relationships have one thing in common: It started with a profound pain that you TOLERATED.

You dismissed the pain and stayed in the relationship for whatever reason. Then, you got used to the pain. The next time it happened, it didn't hurt as much. Soon, it became NORMAL, and you just dealt with it.

You give your strength AWAY when you continue to ignore the pain.

The longer you stay, the weaker you become.

If you remain in this kind of relationship, it will be HARD to leave. You both become codependent. You need and want each other's brand of crazy! It is a dysfunctional situation. This is why it's so hard to leave each other alone – even with all the drama going on that you both hate.

Mistake #8
Thinking things with the AH will get better.

They won't.

This is a harsh reality that you must accept. The sooner you do, the better off you will be.

You must acknowledge that his behavior may never change and devise a plan of how you will cope with it - if you decide to stay.

My prayer is that you will find the strength to leave – once and for all.

Of course, people do grow and change, but who wants to wait around to be the practice field for that to happen?

Don't ever waste your time and energy waiting for an AH to grow up. Do yourself a favor and move on.

Mistake #9
Not recognizing his secret ENVY.

If the AH picks a woman who has more going on for herself than he does in any area of his life, he will likely harbor secret envy.

This is important to know because envy will be the source of the mean-spirited abuse the AH will inflict on her - but she may have no idea as to where it comes from or why.

If your critical thinking, financial, or business skills are more sophisticated than his, you are a threat to his manhood. Remember, he's the smart one in the relationship. He must win at all costs. He can't bear to see someone other than himself in the lead, especially a woman.

His self-worth is so low that he will never want to admit that you are more powerful in any area, (especially finances). He will hide his true feelings regarding any of your abilities that are more advanced than his.

Meet Andrea, 26 Tampa, Fla.

"I once dated an AH whose six-figure plus salary wasn't enough to ease his jealousy of my credit score being higher than his. Even though I didn't make much money, and his investment portfolio far exceeded mine, he couldn't hide his annoyance. I was shocked. It sounds silly, but I could tell that my financial successes really bothered him."

Mistake #10
Not doing enough research or ignoring information from your research.

A friend of mine Chole, 37, a smart, beautiful law school student with a banging body, always plays a game of twenty questions with men she meets as a fun way of screening them.

Their responses to these questions tell her much about them and give her clues as to whether she should proceed to date them.

One gentleman she was extremely interested in; Sean, 42, a muscular, clean-cut (wealthy) businessman, invited her on a lunch date. She met Sean at a charity mixer; they exchanged numbers and agreed to meet the next weekend.

On their first date, Chloe explained the twenties game and its meddlesome questions, which Sean agreed to and seemed curious about. The first round of questions was fun for them both. She boldly asked a question regarding the number of women he had recently been sleeping with and his relationship to them.

Her blunt probing led to an all-out interrogation, which she could tell made Sean uncomfortable. She continued to push, explaining that the nature of the game was to reveal dating compatibility. Her prying changed the whole dynamic of their date, and things were going sour quickly.

She sensed that he was hiding something. Her intuition said he was either a rogue tramp or married and she could not tell which. She quickly dismissed her hunch because Sean had so much to offer. He was a high-value man with a beaming smile and heck, he was sexy.

She realized she had made a fatal mistake. She made light of her nosiness and tried to smooth things over, but she could tell he was turned off.

She pursued the relationship, contacting him and he seemed interested in giving her a second chance. After a few dates she could tell he was not as enthusiastic as he had initially been. She figured it was due to her pushing him for answers regarding his love life. She tried to remedy the situation by being extra flirty and sweet. She wore her best sexy-chic dresses and looked stunning whenever she went out with him.

Months went by, and she continued seeing him against her own better judgment. Things were flowing smoothly, and she wanted to get to know him better, and like I said before, Sean was undeniably FINE, and his pockets were deep, so she would take the risk.

Over the next few months, she had lingering questions about his lifestyle. He always seemed to keep her at arm's length, even though they had a connection like neither of them had ever had before. They always had fun together, the sex was amazing, and they made the perfect couple.

On a random road trip, his mother called on his cell, and he introduced Chloe as a "special friend." All three of them happily chatted. His mom was impressed with Chole, and they became quick friends. Chole spoke to her frequently over the phone and she knew she was his mom's favorite, which was the icing on the cake!

Things were going well, so Chloe chose to forget all the flags and warnings she noticed when she first met Sean and the others that would randomly pop up as she continued to see him. They were beginning to multiply, but she quickly pushed them out of her mind.

Flags, like how he rather enjoyed her walking a few steps behind him, how he dominated their conversations, being more interested in her listening to him – rather than hearing what she had to say.

How he was slightly jealous of her accomplishments, her close to 800 credit score and the fact that she was a boss babe, griding daily on her own business and aggressively pursuing her law degree.

How he disappeared some weekends with the fellas, and it was "understood" that she was not to call or to contact him. How his Facebook account still said "single" even though they had been seeing each other for over six months. She considered them a couple, and when she brought it up to him for discussion, he said nothing about it, nor did he change his FB status.

She was displeased with the fact that he still talked to his ex-girlfriend – and her children. She wondered if he was sending them money, but didn't dare ask, because he acted like it wasn't really any of her business. She watched him closely for signs to reveal if he was still in love with her. Why were they still in contact, since she had broken his heart by breaking it off and was now living with another man – and why in the world would he be sending her kids money?

She couldn't understand why he was annoyed with the looks and attention she received from not just men but women when they were out together. She had always kept herself up; worked out frequently, wore stylish clothing, and her hair, skin, and nails were always on point. She knew she was a pretty girl, so attention from others was normal for her. She couldn't put her finger on what was upsetting about it to him, since people were always polite and respectful. She never gave him any reason to doubt her loyalty.

Lastly, she hated how he and some of his male friends were weirdly close and how sometimes, he just seemed – feminine. She dismissed this since Sean was an alpha male and she loved his sexy expressions of masculinity.

Chloe liked Sean and wanted the relationship to develop into a commitment, but she couldn't help but notice his hesitancy, aloofness, and… quiet envy.

They continued spending time together, and he was falling in love with her. After a year and a half of "hanging out," he gave her a key to his penthouse. She allowed herself to fall in love with him despite her confusion surrounding the fact that he was always available - yet he frequently acted like HE DIDN'T LIKE HER. This was a mystery since they spent all their free time together and got along well.

He took her on dates and expensive trips, and he was good to her, yet she had no idea why he behaved the way he did.

Whenever she brought his wrongdoings to his attention, he was remorseful and patiently listened to all she had to say. He would apologize, say he was sorry and wrong and insist that he would do better in the future. She had no reason not to forgive him and to allow him to make it up to her.

She began to think he was "the one," rationalizing that his Jekyll-Hyde behavior was because he was a man and needed some space to unwind and de-stress. He didn't seem to be mentally ill, or Bipolar, nor was he a narcissist. He genuinely acted like he loved her, was balanced in his thinking, and was loving, kind, and thoughtful - except when he was being a total AH. Chloe was incredibly happy with him – most of the time.

Still, she sensed Sean was holding something against her. She felt like he cared for her, but always had something to nitpick with her about. The way she looked, her eating habits, her hair, etc. She felt like he was trying to control her and noticed that her life had begun to take a strange direction away from the things she loved. His nitpicking and ill comments made her feel like she was ugly and began to tap away at her self-worth. One minute he was sweet, taking her to dinner, spending quality time and talking about their future together. The next he was insulting her and made her feel like she wasn't good enough for him.

Months of hurt after hurt drove her to the reality that the relationship was just too painful to continue. The big blow came when he embarrassed her in front of their friends by posting on Facebook about another woman that he was DATING? - when they had been exclusive for close to a year. Not only had he been seeing this other woman, but it was obvious that everyone knew. Except for Chloe, of course.

Totally wounded, Chloe retreated and refused to see him. It was hard. She couldn't believe that after all this time and after all the trips they had taken together, after they both poured their hearts out to each other, after all the love they made, how could he be so dirty? For him to cheat was one thing, but to blast it on social media was another. She was devastated. It made no sense to her heart, but she knew she had to let go.

Looking back, two years later, Chole now acknowledges that the flags were there from the very beginning. Sean was never honest about the number of women he was dating. It was obvious to her now that he wasn't as into her as she was him and that she was the one who pursued the relationship - when she knew he was ready to walk away.

She saw the signs early on. She concluded Sean was indeed bisexual, hence all the feminine mannerisms and the trips with the boys where she was completely shut out. He never mentioned the trips or even talked about them.

He punished her throughout the duration of their relationship, and she wondered if it was because of a silent guilt that he carried because of his unfaithfulness to her since she was such a pure-hearted, loving person.

Sean obviously didn't want to be with just one woman (or man). She concluded that he was a lowlife. He was spoiled and wasn't ready to settle down. He liked playing house, having sex, and going through the love motions. Not to mention his sexual orientation was up in the air, since she was convinced that he was sleeping with men.

She felt he was playing a game, toying with her mind, enjoying how deeply she loved and cared for him. She believes he had no intention of getting serious with her, that he was just having fun and enjoying his life and money with her. All this made Chloe angry with Sean and she vowed to never give him another chance to use her.

He would faithfully reach out to her, trying to rekindle what they had. Her answer was an emphatic NO. She felt their relationship was sport for him, and he didn't seem saddened by the fact that she was no longer a part of his life. It took Chloe many months to stop crying over Sean. She knew it was her fault. There was no one to blame but herself. She eventually found the strength to stop pining away over him and move on.

Moral of the story?

Be vigilant about your love choices. Flags, whether small or large, appear for a reason. Don't ignore them. Dig deeper to uncover circumstances and situations that could play against you. Walk away when you know you need to do so.

I have pondered Chole's relationship with this man. His dishonesty and her seeing through his surface-level answers seemed to fuel an anger that caused him to quietly lash out at my friend. Perhaps, he was embarrassed by her accurate assessment of his love life and sensed that she picked up on his bisexual habits. Either way, she knew something was off – yet she continued to see him. This proved to be a big mistake, leaving her broken and hurting long after they split.

Mistake #11
Thinking the AH really loves you.

I know he said he loved you.

He's lying.

The AH does not love you, nor is he capable of loving relationships. His life is structured to obtain the three things that are most important to him: Money, Power, and Sex.

Any of these that he feels deficient in, he will work diligently to increase, to avoid feelings of failure. Inadequacy makes him feel feminine, and he is too chauvinistic to surrender to any thought of weakness.

Love requires sacrifice, energy, and time. Love requires commitment, accountability, and consistency. Love requires that you be present. Love requires more than the AH will ever give to any woman. He is accountable only for those things which will increase his supply of the big three – money, power, and sex.

Sacrifice is not something he is accustomed to. His selfish nature resists giving to anything without an immediate payback.

There are many reasons why you should not believe it when he says he loves you. His whole motivation for sticking around is to keep your attention and time focused on him.

When you met him, you were healthier, stronger, and more vibrant. The longer you stay with him, you will become less of who you are and more of the prisoner he planned for you to be.

Mistake #12
Thinking that you can love the AH into changing his self-centered ways.

You cannot change the AHs devilish, self-centered ways.

Extreme circumstances such as loss, death, dire need, and traumatic events change hearts. God changes a wicked heart. Wicked hearts don't just change by themselves. It will take focus, time, and a great deal of dedication to change a wicked AH heart.

It is a mistake for women to think that the AH can reverse his ways at the drop of a hat. He can't and he won't no matter how good your companionship is. Change is a process, and you must be willing to endure the pain and the challenges that will come while waiting for the AH to recover. You must change how you think if you are going to stay with him. You must ACCEPT him the way he is and consent to his off behavior. You must learn to go with the flow – whatever that may be, until he declares that he is ready to end his AH ways, even if it takes a lifetime for him to do it.

Mistake #13
Allowing Yourself to fall too quickly for an AH.

As women, we often allow ourselves to fall in love too quickly. It takes practice and experience to harness emotions and to wait for a new relationship to prove it is a healthy, non-treacherous option.

Don't allow yourself to fall in love with a man who is a high-risk AH candidate with red flags that should not be dismissed. His not being sure of how he feels about you and his dismissive, non-committal behavior is not only a flag, but a huge problem.

We have already planned the wedding based on how we feel – not the status of the relationship or how he actually treats us. Stop yourself from developing feelings until you know that this man is healthy, committed and truly capable of loving you.

Chapter 8

MOVING FORWARD

If you have spent months settling for less with an AH without getting the love, support, and what you really want (a commitment), you're probably ready to end the drama and admit that enough is enough.

You may now be ready to take a hardcore assessment of your relationship and what it will take for you to move on. It has cost time and plenty of heartache to get to this point. If you have decided to stay, then prepare yourself for a tumultuous path of highs and lows. If you have decided to walk away, you are probably heartbroken since a breakup is not what you had hoped for. You must begin to slowly detach. Your dream has come to a screeching halt. Be comforted. It is never worth it to sacrifice your peace, joy, and self-respect for a man, no matter how much promise you think he has.

Move on. Dream again.

Every man is not an AH. There are some very good men out there. It may take some time and effort to find him, but there is someone out there who will love you the way in which you deserve to be loved.

Guard Your Heart

Your heart will try to find a way to keep the AH in your life by excusing and downplaying his negative behavior.

You must remember that his presence is destroying all that you are, and all that God created you to be.

He will not stop. You will continue to be drained of life and strength for as long as he is allowed access to your heart.

Take some time to nurture yourself.

You are on the road to AH detox and recovery. Put yourself on a self-care plan. Pray, cry, relax, heal. Eventually you will and must get back out there in the dating world.

Love awaits you!

Chapter 9

BREAKING FREE

The AH must lose you (really lose you), for him to realize your worth.

He is not a basic narcissist. He is a smarter, more upscale, savvy kind of fellow. He does have a heart, but it is filled with greed. He does not play OBVIOUS mind games. He is fueled by lust. He has the capability to be a very nice person but is still very much a wolf.

He will acknowledge and confess his shortcomings, apologize with all insincerity, and really mean it. He fluctuates between being a sweetheart and the proverbial "DOG."

He is fully aware of his foolish mindset and could choose to be a better person BUT DOESN'T. He's a normal, regular guy who allows his selfishness to guide him for no logical reason.

His desire for acknowledgment and clout exceeds his desire for love and intimacy.

Honestly analyze why your love for this man is stronger than your desire to be healthy. You must understand what it is that you enjoy (or need so badly) that it keeps you going back to him.

Chapter 10

WHAT IS YOUR WHY? AN EXERCISE TO HELP YOU

What makes this man worth staying connected to him? Make a list of all your WHYs. Be 100% honest. You cannot move forward to healing without understanding how and why you arrived at your current relationship condition.

This exercise will help you gain clarity. Search your soul. Remember, the question is why are you staying and what need is being met? Lastly, list how the relationship is helping and hurting you.

I have included some suggestions to help you get started.

Possible Answers to Your Whys:

- ✓ Chemistry. We share a level of intimacy or warm connection.
- ✓ He is easy to talk to and there isn't anyone who understands me like he does.
- ✓ We always have fun together.
- ✓ I don't want to be alone.

My Financial Whys (why do you stay / what needs are met?)

- I stay because:
- My needs that are met:

My Sexual Whys (why do you stay/ what needs are met?)

- I stay because:
- My needs that are met:

My Emotional Whys and Other Whys (why do you stay / what needs are met?)

- I stay because:
- My needs that are met:

Chapter 11

MAKE UP YOUR MIND TO DETACH

The AH possesses a stubborn pride that refuses to yield or show honest emotion.

It may take a lifetime for him to move past the limitations that stop healthy, vulnerable relationships dead in their tracks. These men are broken beyond your ability to help them recover.

You can try, but the choice is his to make to accept the help you so desperately want to give him. You set yourself up for a great deal of suffering trying to nurse him back to wholeness.

My advice? Let someone else do it. The AH needs professional help. Find a man who will change, grow, and do whatever it takes to be part of a balanced, healthy relationship with you. What you need is a partner and a friend. Someone who is willing to share life, with all its hills and valleys, triumphs, and failures.

Chapter 12

WALKING AWAY

At this point, you may be pondering your options in your relationship with the AH:

1. Stay and put up with his clownery.

2. Run away and be free.

3. Stay and walk away slowly.

Number three is a risky decision that I do not recommend but may be necessary in certain situations.

You will prolong your recovery by trying to help the AH work through his many issues. Walking away slowly is a viable option only for someone who has their lifestyle entangled with an AH. Financial dependence, sharing bills, children, or other circumstances may mean you have no other choice but to withdraw from the relationship a bit at a time. You must focus your energy on repairing your self-worth, regaining your strength, and preparing your heart to make an exit. Do this only after you have a solid escape plan and when the time is right.

If you Stay

You must understand that his behavior may get worse. He knows that he has you trapped and that you won't (or can't) leave. He knows how badly you want or need him. He knows that you want a fulfilling relationship, commitment, or marriage. He has calculated the level of baloney he can feed you and what measure of fake love is necessary to keep you around.

I have listed golden rules that will help you when faced with an AH fork in the road as you navigate your way to healing.

Golden Rule1:

Never, ever under any circumstances give the AH (or any man that has not earned through a solid, identifiable commitment) 100% access to your time, emotions, heart, or body.

If you have already made this mistake and are reaping a corrupt harvest – devise a plan of retreat. Bit by bit begin to pull back on your heart investment.

He must never be the focus of your attention – even if you think he deserves it. Begin to disconnect. Boundaries are your friend and biggest defense. Start training yourself to say NO.

Golden Rule2:

Wean your heart from his emotional grip as you prepare to leave. If you have spent considerable time with this man, brace yourself. A heated fight may ensue. Ask God to heal your heart, deliver you from the AHs grip, and to send you someone else. While you are waiting for answers to your prayers, work on a spiritual, mental, emotional, and physical comeback. God always delivers and you can pray for someone with whom you can build and who will love you unconditionally. In the meantime, learn to enjoy your own company and to be okay with being alone until someone better comes along. Fill your time with exercise, study, prayer, and quiet reflection. Get busy!

Golden Rule3:

Stop having sex with the AH. You will know you are stronger when you can say NO. He doesn't deserve your treats. Sleeping with him only cheapens your worth in his eyes. Say no to his requests for your time and attention. You must realize that the AH is your enemy and is trying to stop you from moving forward in life.

If you stick around without setting boundaries and consequences, he will continue abusing you. You must make a list of your boundaries and stick to them.

Don't run to be by his side when he calls. Don't be available. Don't continue in negative conversations that are rude, disrespectful, and just plain mean towards you.

Create a boundary list. Write out what you won't take anymore from the AH. List all things that you know violate your personal convictions, no matter how large or small. Writing them out and reading them on paper will strengthen your heart to say no. I have listed some examples to help you get started.

My AH Boundaries and Consequences:

- I feel disrespected when you swear and interrupt me when I'm speaking. What I have to say is important.

- I will not allow (AH name) to say hurtful words, curse, belittle or love bomb me.

- I will refuse all dates and money offerings that are keeping me bound.

- If you continue to do this, I will end the conversation.

- I will attend the family dinner with your mother and the kids, but I will not attend the holiday party at your office.

- I will say no to any requests for my time, attention, and sex.

Chapter 13

I JUST CAN'T WALK AWAY!

So, you've tried leaving the AH, and you just can't seem to do it. `

You can't because, deep down, you really don't want to.

You are in love, or think you are in love. You are gaining something that you are not ready to give up yet, or you simply don't want someone else to have him.

Remember, this man has been performing this seduction act for a long time. He has become quite skilled at getting what he wants without women noticing that they are being manipulated.

You are no match for his tricks. He recognizes that your talent exceeds his. Your deliverance from his presence would put you in a position to be successful without his influence or permission. He simply won't do the work it takes to possess what he sees in you, even though it is available to all who are willing to do what is required to obtain it. Do you realize that he is using you to catapult his inadequacies to a higher level?

Remember, he is learning from you. He wants you around to continue teaching him. If you leave, he'll work diligently to get you back. Not because he wants you, but because he enjoys using you and doesn't want anyone else to profit from your talents. He only must reign on the throne of your heart.

You must know your worth - some things you CANNOT put up with. You must very calmly insist that he respects you - by walking away. The AH must be managed whether he is a part of your life or not.

If you have moved on you must be careful not to let him back in. If you are married to him, if you don't manage him with boundaries, he will certainly manage you with control. Which would you rather??

Chapter 14

OK, NOW WHAT?

A Checklist of What to do.

You loved him. He played you. You're devastated.

It's going to be okay, but you must do the work to go on with your life.

Here's a daily list to help you.

- ✓ Monitor and adjust your thinking daily. Focus on moving forward.
- ✓ Life will go on without him, Mr. Wonderful is on the way.
- ✓ Make new plans for your future.
- ✓ Be willing to do whatever it takes to walk away and stay away.
- ✓ Stop having sex with him, no matter how badly you want to.
- ✓ Say no to his requests – whatever they may be.
- ✓ Remember, the longer you stay attached, the weaker you will become, and the greater your loss of energy and strength.
- ✓ Block his calls. (Something you must do for your own well-being.)
- ✓ Don't be his friend. He will try to manipulate you into coming back, or even worse, having sex.
- ✓ No email or texting.
- ✓ Unfollow him on all social media / Remove him from your followers.
- ✓ Cut off all contact if you can. If you cannot, limit the time you spend interacting with him. Keep the relationship on a professional level.

✓ Journal. Think. Reflect. Confront your issues head-on. Confront your whys.

✓ Go to new places. Meet new people. See other guys. Duty date, a lot.

Chapter 15

BREAKING THE MENTAL CIRCLE

Walking away is painful. It won't be easy, but it is necessary and DOABLE. Keep moving forward. Things will get better. Do not allow your mind to wander in a mental circle; repeatedly daydreaming about what you and he shared. The conversations, good times, the special moments, the sex…

Here is a quick plan to help you break the circle in what you THINK, DO and SPEAK. Governing your responses in these areas will make your TRANSITION to life without the AH easier.

What you THINK.

Choose what you will think about when your mind is consumed with memories and your heart is aching to talk to or see the AH. Replace thoughts of him with thoughts of scripture, quotes, poems. Do this exercise repeatedly until your mind becomes clear and the AH is no longer the focus of your attention. Be patient with yourself.

What you DO.

Establish new habits and routines while adjusting to being alone. Replace morning and evening habits. Plan new routines and adventures. Get rid of pictures, videos, and souvenirs from your time together. You should avoid anything that leads to reminiscing about old times.

Allow the tears to flow but remember that lengthy crying spells can lead you into further depths of despair. Cry, but do not cry long. Wipe your tears and settle in your heart and mind that you must move forward!

You will miss those daily talks, hugs, or activities together. In those moments, it is crucial to engage in new tasks. This will help to avoid relapsing into negative behaviors such as calling, texting, emailing, or driving by his home or workplace.

What you SPEAK.

Create your environment by speaking what you would like to see. A list of scripture and positive affirmations is an excellent way to frame your day and will help you to get to your destination.

Chapter 16

HOW TO MANAGE A RELATIONSHIP WITH AN A$$HOLE

We have already established that the AH does not like to be challenged, confronted, or exposed. When you begin to express that his behavior is displeasing, expect him to be more than a little upset. AHs do not like boundaries, nor being told what to do. He will not appreciate your disapproval of his leadership style. He may listen quietly with no response or retaliate in the worst of ways. Be prepared for a myriad of emotions: aloofness, silence, angry outbursts, indifference, the cold shoulder, name calling, belittling, insults, arguments, nasty words, or hostility…anything goes.

The next few pages detail what you can do to manage your relationship whether you plan an immediate departure or future exit.

HOW TO MANAGE A RELATIONSHIP WITH AN AH.

1. Commit to a Self-Care Routine.

Commit to a consistent self-care routine immediately if you don't already have one in place. Nurturing yourself right now is necessary for your mental, emotional, and physical well-being. Routine self-care says, "I am important" and is a defense mechanism when your self-love and self-esteem are under attack.

Give yourself a break. Surround yourself with positive people and situations. Meditate, exercise, stay hydrated and eat healthy. Get proper rest and make it a point to treat yourself to some TLC. Every bit of self-care will be needed as you move towards wholeness.

2. Stand Up for Yourself.

Stop agreeing to unfair treatment of yourself. If you are not verbalizing your discomfort with his actions or words, then you agree with them. Take care of yourself first. Remember, giving in to his overbearing demands is how you arrived where you are in the first place.

3. Make a List.

Don't try to engage in conversation with the AH off the top of your head. The AH is used to these kinds of manipulative skirmishes and will try to outtalk you – or worse, downplay what you are trying to say. He may even try to change the subject, confuse you, or change your mind about the topic at hand.

4. Expect emotions to flare.

Your newfound confidence may annoy the AH. He may be angry and lash out at you. Stand your ground. Don't give in to his tantrums or demands. Stay calm, and don't yell or scream. Resist the temptation to get upset. Some AHs are cool and quiet and may not reveal their true feelings, good or bad. Rest assured; he feels some kind of way about your new mindset. Pay attention and wait.

5. Fear Not.

You may be afraid to confront the AH or the situation you are in. It's okay; you don't have to launch a full-scale attack. Take baby steps. Changes in your thinking can begin in silence. Don't allow fear of the AHs responses to arrest your confidence, stop you from communicating or cause you to shut down. Move forward, even in fear, if you must. Sometimes, fear is a warning sign for danger. For life threatening emergencies dial 911. For help, you may contact The Domestic Violence Hotline at 1.800.799.SAFE (7233).

6. You don't have to take the bull.

When did it become okay for you to settle for the bull the AH dishes out? You owe it to yourself to be your own advocate. Purpose in your heart that you will stick to your plan. State your boundaries and enforce them.

7. Remain Calm.

You can't think straight when you are upset. You need to be able to think clearly so that you can communicate your feelings, needs, and wants with clarity. Take deep breaths. Close your eyes and count to 10.

8. Don't interrupt.

Do try to listen calmly as the AH responds. Give him a chance to explain, but do not be swayed by his beguiling words. Remember, one of his finest gifts is manipulation.

Anchor your heart. Whatever he has to say should not affect your decision regarding what is best for you. You must not change your mind based on his pleading, crying, or tricky love bombing tactics.

9. Be Consistent.

Don't put your foot down one day and be a doormat the next. Be consistent in your thoughts, feelings, and actions. Writing things down and having a daily plan will help you. Consistency takes time, but you will gain strength as you create boundaries and enforce them.

10. Speak up.

It is an absolute must that you tell your side of the argument, even if what you will say will upset the AH and disturb the peace.

Some AHs will start a nasty argument at the smell of confrontation, so that they can say, YOU are the cause of the drama. This can happen even if you approach him in a calm, loving manner.

Analyze your message and communication style for areas of weakness before initiating any conversation. While you want to tell him how you feel, you must also be level-headed and fair in the way you state your case. Remember, kindness rules and clarity follows peace!

- Don't be accusatory, demeaning, blaming, aggressive, or overly confrontational in your tone or wording.

- Don't be defensive, picky, or too emotional.

- Write your feelings down. Keep an ongoing list of your concerns. Review your list often to make changes or additions.

- Say the hard things. Don't be afraid to expose the elephant in the room. Sharing your wounds may be just what the AH needs to hear. Say how you really feel, and what you really want. Remember, it is not what you say, but how you say it.

- Do try to be open and understand the AH perspective, even if you know in advance that you don't agree. We are all human. Everyone, even the AH, in all his foolery, deserves a fair chance.

- The AH is who he is. Take it or leave it. Keep in mind he may never change. He needs counseling and spiritual healing. Remembering this will help you stay calm when you would otherwise get angry. You may not always understand why he behaves the way he does and that is okay.

11. Remove Yourself Quietly from a Hostile Environment.

Hostile is not just arguing and yelling. It is any disrespectful words, actions or attitudes that make you feel uncomfortable, violates your self-respect, and steals your peace.

Don't be afraid to say that you need a break and would like to discuss things later. Feel free to excuse yourself when the situation gets nasty.

Some AHs will refuse to let the conversation end and may engage in following you around if you try to leave the room. If you cannot leave, state your case, and then sit quietly. Try to redirect your attention. If leaving is an option, end the conversation politely and walk away, saying as little as possible.

It is very empowering to remove yourself from a heated discussion while using the silent technique. Once you are alone, you can regroup and gather your thoughts for the next meeting.

Do make a list of all you want to say and any questions you have and keep it handy when you speak with him. Stick to 1 or 2 key points for each round of discussion. List everything that you feel needs to be communicated.

Write down ways you can fairly say what you need to say. Go over your list with someone you trust to help you balance your side of the argument. Your list and your friends can help you put things into perspective and reveal areas where you need healing or correction.

12. Check Your Emotions.

Don't allow your low self-esteem, depression, or loneliness to get in the way of your moving forward. Resist the temptation to backslide into negative thought patterns.

13. Say NO.

Give yourself permission to say no. You have the right to say no to anything that makes you feel intimidated, demeaned, or belittled. Don't allow the AH to make you feel as though you are obligated to agree with what he says.

14. Don't Be Afraid to Walk Away.

Sometimes, you must cut your losses and move on, even if it hurts. This may not be feasible for a married woman. In this case, plan an outing. Take a walk. Go outside. Visit a friend. Do something to recharge. Go to your secret place. Refresh, renew. Set your boundaries. Seek counseling. Construct an escape plan and follow through.

15. Continue (or start) Journaling.

Journaling your daily thoughts about life and what you are going through is a great way to relieve stress and sort out your feelings. Writing your goals, fears, and hurts will give you the clarity you need to come up with solutions and release negative thoughts.

16. Create a Place of Escape and a Plan of Exit.

A place to go where you can sit quietly. A place to think, cry, nap, journal, hide (smile). A closet, room, shed, anyplace where you can be alone and be comfortable.

A plan of exit includes destinations, people, places, dates, times, and a financial budget. Map out every detail of your exit strategy. The more prepared and detailed your plan is, the less stressful your departure will be.

17. Shhhhh.

Stop telling his mama, your co-worker, and your big-mouth best friend every detail about your relationship. Move in silence. Find wise people that you can confide in to help you think through your plans. Never post your breakup woes on social media. This is a trap which can make you feel even more lonely and depressed.

18. Rest.

Now comes the hard part. After you have said what needs to be said and are working on your boundaries, here is what you must do next:

- TAKE IT EASY.

- Don't argue. (You have already stated your needs and wants.)

- Remain calm. Don't lose your peace. A clear mind is necessary to continue moving forward.

- Have discussions with the AH when you are most calm.

- Remove yourself from conversations that escalate in a wrong way.

- Don't retaliate. It may feel good but will only cause confusion and strife.

- Listen intently.

- Reiterate your needs calmly, if necessary. Enforce your boundaries.

- Let him vent. You can do this because you are now in a different state of mind. You have a plan, a purpose, and a goal.

- It is okay to not agree with what he says or does. It is okay to say NO.

- Find a trusted friend or therapist that you can vent to.

- Journal any angry, hurt feelings and what you are going through.

- Try not to be agitated. Let peace be your guide.

- Forgive. Let go of any pain or ill feelings towards the AH. This may take time, but you will notice a new level of power and joy rise within yourself. Strength will always come when you stand up for yourself and walk in peace.

19. Reflection time

An exercise for deeper understanding. Grab a pencil and jot your thoughts down.

Think about your first impression of this man.

When, where and how did you meet him? Had you known him before?

What did you love or hate?

How did he make you feel?

What flags did you notice?

What did you find annoying or surprising after your initial encounter?

As you got to know each other, what made you happy or sad?

When did you notice any emotional, mental, or spiritual work that he needed to do?

Did he say or do something that surprised you negatively or positively?

The End